The Ark
and the
Park

The Story of Noah

written and Illustrated by
Damon J. Taylor

KREGEL
Kidzone

FOR PARENTS
with Dr. Sock

This story will help children learn about doing what God wants even when it's not the popular thing to do.

Read It Together–

The story of Noah and the ark is in Genesis, chapters 6–9. Parents may want to read through it on their own first, because Noah does some things that are difficult to explain.

Sharing–

Share with your child about a time when you had to choose between doing what everyone else seemed to be doing and doing what God wanted you to do.

Discussion Starters–

• What would it be like to build an ark when no one had even *heard* of an ark?

• Why is it sometimes difficult to do what God wants us to do?

• Some people have a hard time believing that the story of Noah really happened. Why do you believe that it did?

• What's the biggest boat you ever saw? Would it hold a pair of elephants?

• Do you think Noah thought of all the animals on the ark as his pets?

For Fun–

How many animal sounds can you make? Try playing animal charades.

Draw–

Make a rainbow. Use your imagination. Your rainbows can be posters, or sidewalks, or face paint.

Prayer Time–

Ask God to help you do what's right even when the people around you do not. Thank God for giving us the Bible to tell us what's right.

COLEMAN HAS FOUND THAT THE LIFE OF A LITTLE BOY

can be tough at times, especially if that boy has a baby sister named Shelby. When Shelby was born, Coleman needed a way to deal with his day-to-day problems. He found his socks. Yes, that's right, his socks.

It may seem weird, but these aren't your regular, everyday tube socks that you find in your dresser. As ordinary as they may appear, these socks really are Coleman's friends, and they help him with his problems. When life gets complicated, Coleman goes to his bedroom and works through his troubles by playing make-believe with his socks and remembering Bible stories he's learned.

So please sit back, take off your shoes and socks if you like, and enjoy Coleman's imaginary world in . . .

The Ark
and the
The Park
The Story of Noah

It was lunchtime for Coleman and his school friends. As he always did at lunchtime, Coleman began to pray, thanking God for his lunch.

OKAY, WHICH OF YOU DIRTY SOCKS STOLE MY LUNCH MONEY?

"Dear God, thank you for—"
"Hey, Coleman. Whatcha doin'? Are
you praying for your little lunchy-poo?"
It was Francis, the school bully.

"N-no, Francis, I had something in my eye," said Coleman as he opened his lunch bag.

Coleman didn't like Francis' teasing, but he also knew that thanking God for his lunch was what God wanted him to do.

"What should I do?" asked Coleman as he munched his lunch.

Z-z-z-zip! came the
sound from Coleman's
backpack and out
popped Sockariah,
one of Coleman's
sock buddies.
"Coleman, you
can't let that bully
push you around like
that!" said Sockariah.

"I hate it when he teases me. He makes me feel
goofy for praying," said Coleman as he continued to
eat his sandwich.

"Do you care more about
what others think of you

than what God thinks of you? Don't you remember the Bible story about Noah and the ark?"

"Yeah, but what does a boatful of animals have to do with my lunch?" asked Coleman.

"Just sit back and listen while you eat."

The people of long ago had turned away from
God, and the only person who still obeyed God was
Noah.

"Dear God, thank you for this—"

"Hey Noah, don't tell us you
still pray to God!" laughed
Noah's neighbors.

YOU SEE, LUNCHTIME
BULLIES HAVE EXISTED
AS LONG AS LUNCHTIME
ITSELF.

"Yeah, are you thanking God for your little snacky-wacky?" teased his other neighbor.

Noah continued to pray.

One day when Noah was praying, he heard . . .

DEAR GOD, HELP ME TO DO WHAT YOU WANT ME TO DO.

"Noah!"

"Who said that?" Noah heard a voice, but he could not see anyone.

"Noah," the voice said again. "Noah!"

"Who's there?"

"It's Me."

"Me who?" asked Noah.

"God," the voice answered.

This took Noah by surprise. He had prayed to God all his life, but this was the first time God had spoken back to Noah.

God said to Noah, "Because you and your family love and obey me, I will let you live. The rest of the world has got to go! I am going to send a flood that will wipe the earth clean, and I will start over with your family." God told Noah to build an ark.

"What's an ark?" asked Coleman.
"An ark is a huge boat with many different rooms and decks to live on," said Sockariah.

"Wow, Noah must have had a really big family."

Noah's family really wasn't very big, but the job
God gave to Noah and his sons sure was.

"After we build the boat, you want me to what?!"
asked Noah.

"I want you to fill it with two of each kind of
animal—one male and one female."

"Every animal . . . even skunks?" asked Noah.

"Yes, even skunks," replied God.

"That's a mighty big job," said Coleman. "It would take a long time to build a boat that big."

"It did take a long time. In fact, it took many years to build the ark. It seemed even longer, because all that time Noah's neighbors teased him for obeying God and building a huge boat with no water nearby."

"Hey Noah, what's with the boat? Are you and God going fishing?" They laughed at Noah and teased him.

No one listened to Noah's warnings. The people continued disobeying God and teasing Noah.

Finally, the construction was finished, and all the animals were loaded onto the ark, two by two.

"Hey, Noah, are you and God selling tickets to your floating zoo?" laughed Noah's neighbors as they continued to make fun of Noah and his family.

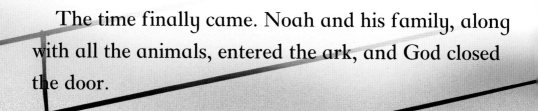

The time finally came. Noah and his family, along with all the animals, entered the ark, and God closed the door.

Noah, his family, and two of each animal were
going to be saved from the flood, just as God had
promised.

Shortly after that, the rain began to fall.

It rained for forty days and forty nights, and the earth was covered with water.

Noah had obeyed God, and God saved the lives of Noah's family and the animals . . . even the skunks. He also put a rainbow in the sky as a promise to never destroy the world with a flood again.

"So Coleman, what do you think? Did you learn anything?" asked Sockariah.

"Well, I learned that an ark is a big boat and that the skunks were lucky to make it onto the ark."

"Anything else?"

"Uh-huh. I learned it's better to please God, like Noah did, than to please others. Like my trying to please Francis instead of God.

"I think tonight when I pray . . . I'll pray for Francis," said Coleman as he finished his lunch. "Great idea, Coleman. Great idea!"

The Child Sockology Series

For ages up to 5
Bible Characters A to Z
Bible Numbers 1 to 10
Bible Opposites
New Testament Bible Feelings

For ages 5 and up
The Ark and the Park: The Story of Noah
Beauty and the Booster: The Story of Esther
Forgive and Forget: The Story of Joseph
Hide and Sink: The Story of Jonah